TOUGH EDDIE

by Elizabeth Winthrop

pictures by Lillian Hoban

E. P. Dutton · New York

Text copyright © 1985 by Elizabeth Winthrop Mahony
Illustrations copyright © 1985 by Lillian Hoban

Library of Congress number 84-13664
ISBN 0-525-44496-3

Published in the United States by
E. P. Dutton, New York, N.Y.,
a division of NAL Penguin Inc.

Published simultaneously in Canada by
Fitzhenry & Whiteside Limited, Toronto

Editor: Julie Amper   Designer: Edith T. Weinberg

Printed in Hong Kong by South China Printing Co.

First Unicorn Edition 1989
10 9 8 7 6 5 4 3 2 1

to Class 4-E, West Side Montessori School, 1982–83

When Eddie wore his cowboy boots and his thick leather belt, he felt tough, all the way to school.

Eddie liked to play in the block corner with
his best friends, Andrew and Philip.

"What are you doing?" Martha asked.

"We're making a spaceship," Andrew said.

"We're going to the moon," said Philip.

"Can I come too?" Martha asked.

"Sure," said Eddie.

"Good-bye, everybody," Philip called.
"Blast off!" Eddie shouted.
They got back just in time to go home
for lunch.

After lunch, Eddie pulled his dollhouse out of the closet. He changed around the furniture in the living room. He set up the children at the kitchen table. It was time for their lunch, too.

Eddie loved his dollhouse. His father had helped him make all the furniture.

That afternoon, when Andrew and Philip
came over, Eddie put the dollhouse back in the
closet.

Eddie and Andrew and Philip shot guns at each
other. They yelled "Hands up" and "Don't move,
or I'll shoot."

They chased each other all around the house.

Eddie's sister, Nellie, was trying to read.

"Be quiet," she said.

"Hands up," Eddie shouted.

"I've got you covered," Andrew yelled.

"Give us all your money," cried Philip.

"Go away and leave me alone," Nellie said.

"Let's tie her up," said Eddie.

Nellie got mad. "If you don't leave me alone,
Eddie, I'm going to tell Andrew and Philip what
you've got in your closet."

"You better not," Eddie shouted.

"What's in his closet?" Andrew asked.

"What's he got?" asked Philip.

"A dollhouse," said Nellie.

"So what?" Eddie said, and he punched his sister in the arm.

"You'll be sorry, Eddie," Nellie yelled as she
ran out of the room.

"You really have a dollhouse?" Andrew asked.

"With dolls in it?" asked Philip.

"Don't move, or I'll shoot," said Eddie.

Eddie's mother opened the door.

"Eddie, put away that gun. It's time for your friends to go home. I don't care how mad you are, you may not punch your sister. Now, go to your room."

The next day, Eddie put on his cowboy boots and his thick leather belt, and he stomped off to school.

Andrew and Philip were waiting for him.

"Do you really have a dollhouse, Eddie?" Andrew asked.

Eddie didn't answer.

"Can we see it sometime?" asked Philip.

"You guys are being mean," Eddie said.

"No, we're not," said Philip.

"I'm not going to talk to you," Eddie shouted.

Eddie played by himself all morning.
Andrew and Philip built a fort in the corner.
Martha painted a picture of the moon.

"It's time to go to the park," the teacher said.
"Choose your partners."
"Will you be my partner, Eddie?" Martha asked.
"Okay," said Eddie.

Andrew and Philip whispered secrets to each other all the way to the park. Eddie felt like kicking them with his cowboy boots.

The teacher put out a plate of apple slices
and cups of orange juice for their snack.
Eddie picked up an apple slice.

"Watch out, Eddie!" screamed Martha.
"There's a bee on your apple."

Eddie didn't move. The bee walked off the
apple slice onto Eddie's hand.

Eddie could see the stinger sticking out of the
bee's tail.

"Just stay still, Eddie,"
the teacher said quietly.

The bee flew up and landed on Eddie's nose.
Eddie closed his eyes. He could feel the bee's
little feet tickling his skin. He wanted to
scream and run away, but he didn't move.

When he heard the bee buzz off his forehead, he slowly opened his eyes. Everybody was looking at him.

"Is it gone?" Eddie asked.

"Yes, it's gone," the teacher said.

"You sure were brave," Martha said.

Eddie smiled. He looked at Andrew and Philip. They were smiling back.

When it was time to go back to school, Andrew grabbed Eddie's hand. Philip and Martha walked in front of them.

"I'm going to bring my pet cricket for show-and-tell tomorrow," Philip said. "What are you bringing, Eddie?"

"I don't know," said Eddie.

"Maybe I'll bring my dollhouse."